KU-033-290

Language consultant: Betty Root

This edition published by Parragon in 2012
Parragon
Queen Street House
4 Queen Street
Bath BA1 1HE, UK
www.parragon.com

Copyright © Parragon Books Ltd 2004

All rights reserved. No part of this publication may be reproduced, stored in a retrieval system or transmitted, in any form or by any means, electronic, mechanical, photocopying, recording or otherwise, without the prior permission of the copyright holder.

ISBN 978-1-4454-6673-6

Printed in China

Give Me a HUG!

Written by Jillian Harker
Illustrated by June Goulding

Bath · New York · Singapore · Hong Kong · Cologne · Delhi
Melbourne · Amsterdam · Johannesburg · Auckland · Shenzhen

$\mathcal{M}$issy was a very daring little mouse. She liked to climb cornstalks, and ...

Wheeeee!

she liked to swing from
willow branches, until ...

one day she fell off!

Crash!

Then Missy didn't feel daring at all.
She stumbled back home to her mum.
"Give me a hug!" wailed Missy.

"Of course I will," said Mum.
She stroked poor Missy's aching head
and, very quietly, she said,

"How's that? Does that take away
the pain? Here's a hug to help you
feel better again."

Then she hugged Missy tight.
And Missy *did* feel better.

Missy was a very
cheerful little mouse.
She smiled as she helped.

She hummed as she played.

But one day, when Missy
lost her favourite teddy bear, she
didn't feel cheerful at all. She
ran downstairs to her mum.

"Give me a hug!" wailed Missy.

"Of course I will," said Mum.
She told Missy to look under
the bed, and when Missy found
Teddy there, Mum gently said,

"I knew you'd find Teddy. You see, I
wasn't wrong. Have a hug and I don't
think those tears will last long."

Then Mum hugged Missy tight.
And Missy began to smile.

Missy was a very brave little mouse.
She liked to sneak up to the farm cat
and tickle his whiskers.

That night,
Missy thought she heard
noises under the bed.

Creak!
Crack!

And she didn't
feel brave at all.

She crept along to her mum.

"Give me a hug!" wailed Missy.

"Of course I will," said Mum.
She took Missy to her room and
looked under the bed. Then, as she tucked
Missy in, Mum smiled and said,
   "Missy, I've looked and I promise you
there's nothing there. Have a hug and
you'll forget all about being scared."

One morning when Mum was really very busy, Missy came running into the room.

"Give me a hug!" she pleaded.

"What's happened now?" asked Mum.

Missy smiled.
"My head isn't hurting.
I don't have a pain.

"I promise I haven't
lost Teddy again.

"I'm not scared
or worried.

"It's just ... well, you know.
Your hugs make me happy.
I do like them so."

"That's good," said her mum, "because ...

"I like it when you ask me if I'll hug you.
Our hugs are the best thing ...

and I love them too!"